W9-ANH-970

The Case of
the Midnight Rustler

John R. Erickson

Illustrations by Gerald L. Holmes

Viking

VIKING
Published by the Penguin Group
Penguin Putnam Books for Young Readers, 345 Hudson Street, New York, New York
10014, U.S.A.
Penguin Books Ltd, 27 Wrights Lane, London W8 5TZ, England
Penguin Books Australia Ltd, Ringwood, Victoria, Australia
Penguin Books Canada Ltd, 10 Alcorn Avenue, Toronto, Ontario, Canada M4V 3B2
Penguin Books (N.Z.) Ltd, 182-190 Wairau Road, Auckland 10, New Zealand

Penguin Books Ltd, Registered Offices: Harmondsworth, Middlesex, England

First published in the United States of America
by Maverick Books, Gulf Publishing Company, 1992
Published by Puffin Books, a division of Penguin Putnam Books for Young Readers, 1999
Published by Viking, a division of Penguin Putnam Books for Young Readers, 2000

1 3 5 7 9 10 8 6 4 2

Copyright © John R. Erickson, 1992
All rights reserved

The Library of Congress has catalogued the Puffin edition as follows:
Erickson, John R., date
The case of the midnight rustler / John R. Erickson ;
illustrations by Gerald L. Holmes.
p. cm.
Previously published: Houston, Tex.; Maverick Books, c1993.
(Hank the Cowdog ; #19)
Summary: Hank the Cowdog investigates the mystery of a cattle rustler
who works by night.
ISBN 0-14-130395-6 (pbk.)
[1.Dogs Fiction. 2. Ranch life —West (U.S.)—Fiction.
3. West (U.S.) Fiction. 4. Mystery and detective stories. 5. Humorous stories.]
I. Holmes, Gerald L., ill. II. Title. III. Series: Erickson, John R., date Hank the
Cowdog ; # 19.
[PZ7.E72556Cami 1999] [Fic]—dc21 99-19586 CIP

Viking ISBN 0-670-88426-X

Hank the Cowdog® is a registered trademark of John R. Erickson.

Printed in the United States of America
Set in New Century Schoolbook

Without limiting the rights under copyright reserved above, no part of this publication
may be reproduced, stored in or introduced into a retrieval system, or transmitted, in
any form or by any means (electronic, mechanical, photocopying, recording or otherwise), without the prior written permission of both the copyright owner and the above
publisher of this book.

This book is dedicated to
James and Shirley Dobson,
in appreciation for their efforts
to save the American family.
God bless them.

CONTENTS

CHAPTER ONE

A New and Exciting Mystery Unfolds

It's me again, Hank the Cowdog. This mystery just might win the prize for chills and thrills, for you see, it gets me involved with a genuine cattle rustler who stole cattle and slipped around in the deep dark of the night and did things that came very close to scaring the liver right out of me.

So get yourself prepared. Do some push-ups. Drink some vinegar and water. Suck on a lemon. Walk around in a circle and say to yourself, "I am NOT going to let this story scare the liver out of me, because living without a liver is worse than no liver at all."

Say that five hundred times and maybe you'll be ready.

Okay, here we go. It all started one morning in the late spring—May, I think it was. Yes, it was around the first of May, or maybe it was the middle of May. Or the end of May.

Let me think here. We'd had our spring round-up and branding, as I recall, and the cowboys were trying to get the first cutting of alfalfa out of the field, and we can pretty well date it from that: the first week in June, just as I suspected.

It all started one morning in June, over in the alfalfa field. Slim and Loper had mowed, raked, and baled half of the alfalfa, and we were trying to get the bales hauled out of the field.

Sally May and Baby Molly drove the old truck, while Slim pitched the bales and Loper stacked. Drover, Little Alfred, and I were in charge of checking beneath each bale for lizards, snakes, crickets, and mice, but especially mice.

It was a happy time on the ranch. Everything was going well. The boys had cut the hay just right, while it was tender and in the bloom. The windrows hadn't been rained on. The machinery was working. The mice were under control. And it was a beautiful morning.

The boys were dripping sweat but happy and working hard, and while they worked they sang an old church hymn they had converted into their

Official Hay Haulers' Song. It was called "See the Morning Sun Ascending."

See the morning sun ascending,
Radiant in the eastern sky.
Hear the angel's voices blending
In their praise to God on high.

Alleluia, alleluia.
Alleluia, alleluia.

I won't say it was a great job of singing. Slim and Loper had their little talents but nobody had ever accused them of being great singers. Still, the song fit the mood and rhythm of the work, and somehow it made us all forget about the sweat and blisters and sore muscles that just seem to be a part of alfalfa hay.

Once we got the bales hauled, it was time to mow down the other half of the alfalfa. Slim climbed on the tractor, made half a round, and broke down.

The mower had thrashed a bearing, several sickle blades, and other items too numerous to mention. And at that very moment, the entire ranch was plunged into darkest gloom and despair.

You ever spend any time around a cowboy

who's forced against his will to repair farm machinery? It's no fun, let me tell you. No more singing, fellers. All at once everyone on the ranch is wearing a long face and kicking things and going around MAD.

Broken machinery seems to have a bad effect on a cowboy's disposition. That's especially true on our outfit because all of the machinery is junk.

Now, if I was running the ranch, I'd go out and buy some haying equipment that stayed in one piece and actually WORKED—you know, tractors that didn't leak water and oil and grease and diesel fuel, and didn't have to be pulled every time you wanted to start 'em.

And a mower that didn't eat bearings for breakfast every day. And a baler that could tie ten bales in a row without being overhauled. And a hay truck with brakes.

Little things like that.

But did the cowboys ask my opinion? Oh no! I was just a dumb dog, and what did I know about running a ranch? So they kept their junky old farming equipment, and every year at haying season we witnessed the same wreck, the same mad scramble to patch up the machinery, and the same long faces.

We dogs might be dumb, but no dog in history

has ever tried to farm 30 acres of alfalfa hay with equipment that ought to be in a museum or a junkyard.

I'll say no more about it, except that if they had listened to the Head of Ranch Security, things would have gone a whole lot smoother.

So there we were, in the midst of our annual Farm Equipment Wreck. Slim and Loper hauled the mower over to the machine shed and tore into it.

What we had was two cowboys, stomping around the machine shed in greasy clothes, baseball caps, and lace-up boots. And mad? They hardly spoke to each other, but they did quite a bit of speaking to the machinery, which was spread out in a thousand parts on the cement floor.

Here's what I mean:

Slim: "Stupid sickle blades! The way they break off, you'd think we'd been mowin' redwood trees instead of alfalfa."

Loper: "The guy who engineered this mess must have been drunk for two months."

Slim: "Too bad there ain't a Tooth Fairy for busted sickle blades. We'd be rich."

Loper: "The way this piece of junk eats bearings, we ought to buy stock in Timken."

Slim: "I'm sure proud I signed on with a COWBOY outfit."

Yes sir, the atmosphere was pretty tense. I was lying down just outside the door, watching Slim as he kicked and talked to various parts of the mower, and wondering if Loper knew that he had a big smudge of grease on the end of his nose, when all at once the cat arrived on the scene.

I glared at him and noticed that the folds of skin that covered my teeth had begun to twitch. I can't explain why that happens, but every time Pete enters the picture, my mouth and lips move into Snarling Mode.

Have I mentioned that I don't like cats? I don't like cats, have no use for 'em at all. They're about as useless as a hog in a hospital. All they do is eat and purr and rub and make a nuisance of themselves.

Well, old Slim was bent down over the sickle bar, whamming on it with a ball-peen hammer. A fly was buzzing in his ear and big drops of sweat dripped off the end of his nose. Pete came gliding across the floor, purring like a refrigerator and holding his tail straight up in the air, and he started rubbing up against Slim's leg.

"Get away, cat."

As you may know, cats don't take hints. They seem to think that everybody loves them and is just waiting around for a chance to become a rubbing post. Pete rubbed and purred and meowed.

"GET AWAY, CAT."

Slim picked him up and pitched him over in Loper's direction. Loper was squatted down on the floor, staring at his project of the moment, which looked like what you'd have if you stuck two sticks of dynamite in a bearing housing and lit the fuse. His lips were forming words but no sounds came out.

Any dog with a brain in his head would have read the warning signs and kept his distance, but do you suppose Pete saw any of that? Oh no. What he saw was something else to rub on, and that's just what he did.

I sure liked what Loper did. Instead of yelling at the cat or erupting in a childish outburst of temper, he reached for the air wrench nearby, hit the button with his finger, and tried to unscrew Pete's tail with a ¾-inch socket.

Hee hee, ha ha, ho ho! I loved it. I'd never realized that Pete could move so fast, but he sure did. The last we saw of the cat, he was heading south at a high rate of speed.

Slim looked up from the mess he was making with the sickle blades and said, "Loper, you ain't much for fixing hay equipment, but I believe you own the patent on fixin' cats."

I barked and thumped my tail on the floor. Loper's eyes came up and speared me. "Hush, Hank, you might be next."

I, uh, decided to keep my opinions to myself.

It was then that my ears picked up the sounds of an approaching vehicle. By the time I could scramble, bark, and move into the Hair Lift-Up procedure, the trespasser's pickup had already pulled up in front of the machine shed.

I hate being surprised and caught off guard, so to make up for lost time, I threw all my reserves of extra energy into the barking maneuver.

In that kind of situation, the very future and survival of the ranch often depends on the courage of its Head of Ranch Security. It's no place for a shrunken violet, I can tell you that, and it's no place for a chicken-hearted little nincompoop like Drover, even though he had beat me to the punch and was out there yipping at the intruder.

But mere yipping is no substitute for the kind of deep ferocious barking that is something of a specialty with me, and when the intruder dared to step out of his pickup and walk toward my machine shed, well, hey, I bristled the hair on my back and bared my fangs and . . .

I'm not going to tell you what happened next, because it wasn't funny AT ALL.

You'll just have to wonder about it, forever and ever.

CHAPTER TWO

Okay, Maybe I'll Tell, If You Promise Not to Laugh

What a cheap trick. If Loper had wanted me to stop barking, couldn't he have just said so? I would have been glad to ... but no, he being a comedian and a humorist and a childish prankster, he had to sneak up behind me and BUZZ ME ON THE BOHUNKUS WITH THAT STUPID AIR WRENCH!!

I thought I'd been shot with a death ray, and no, it wasn't funny when I tried to escape and ran into the side of the machine shed.

It wasn't funny at all, and if I catch you laughing at my misfortune, I'll ... I don't know what I'll do.

11

Yes I do. I'll hold my breath until I'm dead, graveyard dead, and then you'll be sorry. Nobody ever misses a good loyal dog until he's gone, and then they cry and wish they could take back all the mean and hateful things they did to him, but they can't because it's too late.

It was a cheap, shabby trick, and I left a print of my nose in the side of the machine shed, and yes, it did hurt.

How much sympathy did I get from the small-minded people who had witnessed the tragedy? You can guess. Very little. None. I thought Slim and Loper would pass out from lack of oxygen, they laughed so hard.

Had I laughed at their problems? Made fun out of their pathetic attempts to fix up the mower? No, but that didn't stop them from . . . oh well.

This job pays the same, whether they're patting you on the head or making you the butt of their laughingstock.

In typical childish cowboy fashion, they found great pleasure in my misfortune. Fine. I didn't care. Through watering eyes, I glared daggers at them. Someday they would be sorry, and until then . . .

Drover arrived at that very moment. "Hi Hank. Did you just hear a loud crash?"

I gave him a withering glare. "I WAS the loud

crash, you moron, and you're just lucky I wasn't killed."

"Boy, that was lucky. What happened?"

"The owner of this dismal place set off an air wrench under my tail, and I came within inches of destroying the entire south side of the barn."

"I'll be derned. That's quite a tale."

"Thanks. It's the best one I've ever had."

"Oh, I don't know. You've had some pretty good ones."

"No, this is the original equipment, Drover. It's been through some hard times, and there's a tale behind every misfortune it's seen."

"Yep, there's a tail behind every dog."

"Exactly. But dead dogs have no tales."

"Yeah. I wonder what they do with all of 'em."

"Oh, they're passed down from generation to generation and become part of our collective folklore. One of these days, Drover, our children will be telling of our adventures."

"I don't have any."

"That's because you're too chicken. Chickens miss out on all the adventures."

"I mean children."

"Chickens have children, Drover, but no adventures. Chicken children are called 'chicks.' They're hatched from eggs."

"Boy, I love eggs."

"And mother chickens love their children."

"Yeah, but I don't have any. And even if I did, they wouldn't want my tail. It's too short."

"Actually, Drover, the shortest tales are often the best. There's an art to telling a story in just a few words."

"Gosh, Hank, that's the first nice thing you've ever said about my tail. Always before, you made fun of it. Thanks."

"You're certainly welcome." I stared at him for a moment. "Are we involved in the same conversation?"

"I'm not sure."

"Drover, sometimes when I talk to you, I begin to wonder if I'm going insane."

"Yeah, I've wondered about that myself."

"Let's just drop it. Who is this trespasser who just pulled up in the strange pickup?"

"I don't know, but I sure barked at him."

"You barked at him, Drover, but he came on the ranch anyway. You need to work on your barking. You couldn't scare a flea on a grandpa's knee." All at once he sat down and began scratching his left ear. "Don't scratch while I'm talking to you."

"I've got a flea."

"Of course you do. If you'd work on your bark-ing, you wouldn't have so many . . ."

By George, all at once I had a flea problem myself. I could feel the little wretch crawling around on my . . . hee hee, ha ha . . . on my belly, and it tickled. I jumped into the air, bent myself double, and spun around in a circle, trying to catch up with my . . .

You know what? As long as a dog runs in cir-cles, he can never catch up with his own anatomy. It keeps moving, see. You have to shut everything down, sit on the floor, and attack the stupid flea with teeth and lips. That requires deep concen-tration and large amounts of self-deception.

Self-discipline, I should say.

I got 'er done, but it was no easy deal. I bit the flea and the flea bit the dust, and at that point I was ready to pursue the investigation.

Who was this guy who had dared to drive his pickup onto MY ranch in broad daylight? I began by observing that he was an older man, maybe 65 or 70. He walked slowly, wore a battered felt hat and khaki pants and shirt.

His name was Uncle Johnny. I knew that be-cause Loper said, "Well, by gollies, Uncle Johnny! What brings you over here to the poor side of the county? And how are you at fixing hay mowers?"

Uncle Johnny studied the mess on the floor. "Was anybody killed in this wreck?"

"Not yet," said Slim, "but if Loper's disposition don't improve, he's liable to become the first casualty. He gets kind of snarly during hay season, and he wasn't real sweet to start with."

Uncle Johnny chuckled to himself. "Yes sir, I used to get that-a-way myself. Old age don't have too many blessings, but one of 'em is that you can leave the hay work to them that's young and dumb enough to take it."

"Well, we ain't so young," said Slim, "but we've doubled up on the dumb."

Whilst they were making small talk, I decided to slip outside and attend to the routine business of applying our ranch's trademark on Uncle Johnny's tires. A guy never knows when that trademark will come in handy. It's something we try to do every time a strange vehicle comes onto the place.

I had completed my work on the two front tires and was on my way to the left rear when I heard an odd sound. I stopped and listened. There it was again. It sounded like ... I wasn't sure what it sounded like.

The last gasps of a drowning victim? A diesel engine that needed some repair work?

It appeared to be coming from the bed of the pickup, so I slipped around to the rear, went into a deep crouch position, leaped up into the back end, and landed right in the middle of something huge and hairy.

Yikes, what was that thing? A huge fur coat? A dead horse? Whatever it was, it had a head, a BIG head, and it rose from the dead, so to speak, and revealed two sleepy eyes. For a long, tense moment, I stared at it and it stared back at me.

At last I was able to fight back my feelings of shock and surprise and say, "I don't know who you are, fella, but don't get any smart ideas. We've got this place surrendered." I stared at him. "Surrounded, I should say. Holy smokes, are you a horse or a dog?"

I mean, this guy was HUGE!

He grinned and yawned and spoke in a slow voice. "Howdy. Name's Brewster. Where we at?"

"You're in the back of someone's pickup, Brewster, but also on my ranch. That's the part that concerns me. I'm the Head of Ranch Security, you see."

"Aw heck. Last thing I knew, we were in front of Uncle Johnny's house. I guess I fell asleep." He yawned again. "Takes a lot of sleep to keep this old body percolatin'."

"Yes, that's a large body, Brewster."

"Thanks. Everybody says that. I don't feel all that big, but I guess I am."

"You are, believe me. I'd guess you've got some St. Bernard in you somewhere. I'm not the kind of guy who talks about other dogs having big feet, but those feet of yours are really something."

"Yeah." He stood up and stretched. "They always said that I got my big feet and gracefulness from the St. Bernard side, and my ferocious disposition from the German Shepherd side."

He grinned and yawned again. That made about three yawns in the space of three minutes. Then he lumbered over to the endgate of the pickup, and in the process of doing that, he bumped into me and stepped on my foot.

It felt like I'd been stepped on by an elephant and run over by a truck. I squalled.

He gave me a sleepy look. "Oops, sorry. I'm a little awkward first thing in the morning. Takes me a while to wake up."

"Hey Brewster, it's not the first thing in the morning. It's going on ten o'clock, and around here, we figger the day's half over at ten o'clock."

"Yep, and if a guy's going to catch himself a nap, he ought to do it in the middle of the day."

He lumbered back to his spot at the front of

the pickup, stepped on my foot again, and flopped down. The whole pickup shook when he bedded down. He crossed his paws in front of him and rested his chin on the paws. Then his eyes appeared to roll back in his head.

"Just one moment, Brewster. I have some questions I'd like to . . ."

"Skaw, snork, skrunk, zzzzzzzzzzz."

The window of opportunity had slammed shut. Brewster was asleep again.

CHAPTER THREE

Chosen for a Dangerous Assignment

So there I was, looking down at a sleeping horse in dog's clothing, and I still didn't know what he was doing on my ranch. I wasn't much inclined to wake him up again. I mean, this dog was obviously a threat to the health and safety of everyone around him. He could land a guy in the vet clinic just by walking across the room.

Those were the biggest feet I'd ever seen, and boy, did they HURT when they stepped on you!

I left him where he lay and returned to the machine shed, in hopes that I might be able to listen in on Uncle Johnny's conversation and piece together a motive for his presence on my ranch.

I knew there was a motive somewhere, had to be. For every action, there's a reaction. For every auto, there's a motive. Uncle Johnny's auto was still parked in front of the machine shed, and my next assignment was to do a little automotive research on the sly.

I slipped into the machine shed on feet that were trained to make no sound whatever, and took up a position in the shadows. For the next several minutes I monitored the conversation, and soon a pattern began to develop.

Piece #1 of the Puzzle: Uncle Johnny was summering 60 head of cows with calves in a pasture called "The Canyon Pasture," which joined our outfit on the north end.

Piece #2 of the Puzzle: This so-called "Canyon Pasture" was so called because it had a big canyon running through the middle of it. A lot of dogs would have missed this detail, but I picked it up right away. See, if they'd called it the "Creek Pasture," that would have indicated that ... well, maybe you get the picture.

Piece #3 of the Puzzle: Uncle Johnny had been coming up short on his calf count and ... here comes the shocker, so get ready ...

Piece #4 in the Puzzle: He had begun to suspect that someone or something was STEALING HIS CATTLE.

After he had made this incredible revelation, seven eyes stared at him in disbelief. Seven eyes?

That sounds odd, doesn't it, and there aren't too many ways you can get an odd number of eyes looking on in disbelief. Hang on a second while I run a spreadsheet on this and use some Heavy Duty Math and refigger the count. Let's see:

Loper................. two
Slim.................. two
Me.................... two

Two + Two + Two = 3t + 3w + 3o/t + w + o = 3 + 3 + 3 = 6

Okay, six eyes stared at him in disbelief. Boy, I'll tell you, in the Security Business we'd be lost without spreadsheet analysis and Heavy Duty Math. We use 'em every day, and I hope the kids will take notice of this.

Learn that math, kids. It's very important, especially if you want to go into crinimal work. Well, not exactly crinimal work. That suggests that we're crinimals, which we're not. Far from it. We're working AGAINST the crinimals, and if you want to work against the crinimals, you'd better get your math.

Where was I?

Talking about careers, I guess. Careers are very important, and when you're sliding down the banister of life, be careful not to get a splinter in your career.

A little humor there, but I still can't remember what I was talking about. Sometimes we use humor to conceal the fact that . . .

It really annoys me to launch into an important discussion and then forget the dadgummed subject, makes a guy sound about half-goofy.

Oh boy.

This has never happened to me before, honest.

I'll get it here in just a second.

This is embarrassing.

Okay, I've got it now. Here we go. Seven eyes stared at Uncle Johnny in disbelief. Loper was the first to speak.

"That's a pretty serious charge. There's lots of ground between a short count and cattle theft. I'd like to think we don't have any rustlers around here."

Uncle Johnny nodded. "I know it's serious, but I've ridden all the outside fences and they're all in good shape. And I rode upon some tire tracks yesterday."

"Uh-oh."

"That's what I thought too. Uh-oh. They were made by a pickup and a stock trailer, and they weren't mine. Boys, somebody's been slipping into my pasture at night and stealing my calves. I don't want to believe it, but there she is."

Loper pulled up a paint bucket and sat down. "What do you intend to do about it?"

Uncle Johnny said that he'd already called the Cattle Raisers inspector and told him to be on the lookout for calves in the UJ brand. Then he hitched up his khaki pants.

"Loper, it's been a while since I put one of these mowers back together, but I think I could do it."

Loper studied him. "You jumped subjects there, Johnny. Was there supposed to be a step or two between cow thieves and fixing this mower?"

Uncle Johnny narrowed his eyes and grinned. "I thought you might catch that. Here's my deal. If I help you get this mower into the field, maybe you can spare old Slim for a little moonlight work."

Slim's brows jumped three inches on that. "Whoa now, hold on just a minute. What's moonlight work?"

Uncle Johnny explained his idea. Slim would load a packhorse with camping gear and ride up into the canyon, make camp in an isolated spot, and wait for the rustlers to strike again. Since he wouldn't be taking a pickup, there would be no fresh tire tracks to alert the rustlers.

Pretty slick idea, seemed to me.

"Yeah, well, there's one little detail that bothers me," said Slim. "Bein' a range detective ain't one of my many skills, and I've got a natural aversion to gettin' myself shot."

"Oh phooey, you ain't going to get shot. You don't have to catch 'em, son, just get close enough to take down a license number and a description of their pickup. The brand inspector can take it from there."

"Well . . ."

"It'll be easy as pie. All you have to do is lay around camp and sleep until they come."

"Now, I can handle that part."

"You got a good dog?"

Slim's gaze found me in the shadows. I held my head high and wagged my tail. By George, they wanted a good dog? Well, there I was, and it was about time somebody took notice.

Slim shook his head. "Nope, just Hank."

"There you go. He'll bark and let you know when somebody's in the pasture. Until then, all you have to do is lay back and take life easy—and think about me and Loper down here, trying to get this mower put back together."

"It's sounding better and better. I believe me and moonlight work could learn to get along."

Loper slapped his hands on his knees and stood up. "You've got yourself a deal. Slim, throw some camping gear together and have your camp set up before dark. We'll slap this mower together and maybe I can get the alfalfa laid down tomorrow morning, before it dries out."

"What'll I use for a packhorse?"

Loper thought about that for a minute. "Why don't you use that three-year-old colt?"

"He ain't broke, is all."

"He will be, by the time you get to the canyon. That would be the best thing in the world for that old colt. What do you have to lose?"

Slim rolled his eyes. "Oh, let's see: my life, my clothes, my pride, my reputation . . . little things like that."

"Well, it's the little things that count, so I know you'll be careful." Suddenly Loper's smile disappeared. "Slim, there's only one thing about this deal that bothers me."

"Oh?"

He placed a hand on Slim's shoulder and looked him in the eye. "It won't be easy to carry on this farming without your expert advice and cheerful attitude."

"I'll bet."

"But I can accept that. I can even accept the possibility that once you get a packsaddle on old Jughead, he might jump off into the canyon and take you with him."

"Uh-huh."

"Those are acceptable risks, just part of the honor of being a cowboy."

"Yalp. Get to the point, Loper, I'm dying to hear this."

"Slim, the part that really bothers me is that you'll be taking my wife's favorite dog up into the canyons, on a dangerous assignment."

"I see, uh-huh."

"And I hope you understand how broken-hearted she'd be if anything was to happen to her beloved Hank."

My goodness, I had never expected . . . I'd never dreamed that Sally May felt so strongly about, well, ME. I mean, let's face it. She and I had gone through some moments of tension and stress, and on more than one occasion I had been the victim of a misunderstanding.

But hey, let me tell you. Loper's words almost brought tears to my eyes. Suddenly I forgot all the rocks she'd thrown at me, all her cutting remarks about my "odor," as she called it, all the tacky and hateful words she'd said in anger.

Right then and there, I forgave her everything—because I knew that she really CARED. That means a lot to a dog, and I made a note to myself to give her an extra big juicy lick on the ankle the next time we met. Or maybe even on the face.

Well, it was a very emotional moment for Slim and Loper, I could see that. Their loyal dog and Head of Ranch Security was going off on a dangerous assignment, and . . . well, that's pretty heavy stuff.

Slim nodded his head and, that was odd, seemed to be biting one side of his lip. "Tell Sally May that I'll guard him with my life. Come on, pooch, we've got things to do and places to go."

Sally May
Punches My Face

With my head held high, I fell in step beside Slim and we marched out of the machine shed.

It was a moving experience, a cowboy and his trusted dog going out into the Great Unknown to fight for the ranch and protect it from evil forces. I could almost hear the band playing our battle song—drums, trumpets, cymbals . . . laughter?

Hmm, that was odd. I was almost sure that my ears picked up the sounds of laughter coming from the machine shed. I couldn't imagine why Loper and Uncle Johnny would be laughing in the midst of such a solemn ceremony. I mean, it seemed a little out of place to me.

But as long as they were laughing and happy, who was I to complain? I had received the highest honor a dog can ever hope for—heartfelt expressions of appreciation and adoration—and that was good enough for me. Shucks, I was ready to go out and eat a couple of cattle rustlers for dinner.

Just then, Drover came padding up, "Hi, Hank. Are you going somewhere?"

"That's correct."

"Can I go too?"

"Sure, Drover, we'd be glad to have you along."

He began hopping around in circles. "Oh boy, I'm all excited about this."

"I noticed."

"It gets kind of boring around here sometimes."

"Wherever you are, Drover, it gets kind of boring."

"Yeah, I hope it's not just me."

"Oh no, surely not."

"Thanks, Hank. Where we going?"

"Up into a deep dark canyon to catch a gang of bloodthirsty cattle rustlers."

Now get this. All of a sudden, and I mean instantly, it appeared that Mister Stub-Tail suffered a blowout on his left front leg. We're talking about pain and agony and crippled for life.

"Oh, drat the luck! This old leg picks the very worst times to go out on me. Maybe I'd better stick around here. I just don't think I could stand the pain."

I kept walking. "I know you'll hate to miss another big adventure."

"Yeah, it's terrible, being an invalid all the time." He began backing toward the machine shed. "It'll be boring around here, but I'll do my best to take care of things. Bye, Hank, and be careful."

I didn't bother to say good-bye. Drover is so predictable. Sometimes I think ... oh well. We'd be better off without him anyway.

Slim had parked his pickup down by the gas tanks, and it appeared that we were headed in that direction. We marched down the hill, past the yard gate, and on to the gas tanks. Slim removed the lid from the pickup's tank and began filling it with gas, and I saw my opportunity to take a quick dip in Emerald Pond—my own private name, by the way, for the overflow of the septic tank.

On a hot summer day, there's nothing quite as refreshing as a plunge into those healing waters. My coat of hair gets very hot in the summertime, don't you see, and I can say without exaggeration that Emerald Pond has saved my life on more than one occasion.

I went sprinting to the water's edge and dived into its green embrace. Oh, wonderful coolness! Oh, manly fragrance! I relaxed my legs and surrendered my whole entire being to cool floatinghood.

It was then that I noticed Sally May coming down the path from the corrals. It was OUR dog path she was using, if you want to get technical about it, but I sure didn't have any problem with her borrowing it for a while. Sally May is welcome to use our path any time she wants.

Walking with her that morning was Baby Molly, age one year or thereabouts. It appeared that Molly was learning to walk on two legs, and I've often wondered why we dogs never learned that trick.

How do you explain that? Both Little Alfred and Molly had started out walking on all fours, just the way a normal dog would do it, but then at some point they switched over to the two-legged approach.

It makes me wonder if I missed a lesson or two in my early training. How come I can't do that? I've tried it many times, but I could never go more than a few steps on two legs.

Beats me. Maybe that's just the way it's supposed to be, but it does make a guy wonder.

Anyways, there was Sally May, the very lady who, according to our intelligence reports, would be worried sick about me while I was on combat duty up the in the deep dark canyon.

Yes, I was a very busy dog. Yes, I had many things on my mind as I prepared to go into combat against the Deadly Gang of Rustlers. But one of the marks of a true Head of Ranch Security is that he MAKES time for the important people in his life.

I mean, in this line of work, a guy can get so wrapped up in his own affairs that he forgets to share himself with the very ones he's protecting out there on Life's Front Lines. At some point you just have to by George stop and smell the rose-colored glasses.

The opportunity had presented itself for me to spend some quality time with Sally May and her little daughter, so I hauled my wet and highly conditioned body out of Emerald Pond and loped over to them.

When I arrived, Sally May was kneeling beside Baby Molly and appeared to be engrossed in something. Oh yes. Molly held a big black bug in her fist and was trying to eat it.

(Let me pause here to mention that, in some ways, Molly was a weird little kid. I mean, she ate things like dirt and leaves and twigs. And bugs. Shucks, I once saw her chewing on the trunk of a tree. Can you imagine that? A little girl trying to eat a whole tree? Maybe she was part beaver, I don't know.)

Anyways, she had this black beetle clutched in her plump little fist, and she'd already made up her mind to eat that rascal, but Sally May had other ideas and was trying to pry open her fist.

I figgered this might be a good time for me to shake all the loose water out of my coat. Every once in a while we dogs will drip-dry, but it's usually better to shake. It's a little more trouble but better in the long run.

Cuts down on the chances of getting the sniffles. As much as we use our noses in the Security Business, we sure don't need the sniffles.

So I closed my eyes, extended my tail, and went into the shaking maneuver, shook every inch of hair and tissue between the tip of my nose and the end of my tail. It was a heck of a good shake, but suddenly the peace and tranquility of the moment were interrupted by a piercing scream.

Over the years I have observed that for every scream, there is a screamer. That scream didn't just happen. It had been caused by something, and I had a pretty good idea what it was.

Sally May had gotten a good look at that bug and it had scared the daylights out of her.

Well, you know where I stand on the matter of Ladies in Distress. Nothing in this world calls me into action quicker than the scream of a lady in distress, especially if she happens to be my master's wife.

In a flash, I had cancelled the Shake Program and had gone into Manual Hair Lift-Up and switched over to Double Baritone Bark. Pretty impressive, huh? But that wasn't all. In the midst of all this switching of programs and circuits, I somehow found an opening of time to leap into Sally May's lap and give her my biggest, juiciest, most comforting lick on the face.

How did I manage to accomplish all of that in the space of just a few seconds? I can't tell you. Somehow it all comes together at the right time. It goes back to our rigorous training, I suppose.

Training, self-discipline, physical conditioning, and the kind of protective instincts you expect to find in a top-of-the-line cowdog.

I have no idea why she turned on me like she did. I mean, we're talking about wild eyes and flared nostrils and clenched teeth, and do you believe that she actually SLUGGED ME ON THE NOSE?

Yes sir, delivered a roundhouse right that landed between my nose and upper teeth. I never would have believed that a proper lady would actually slug a dog, but this one did.

She gave a howl of pain and began shaking

the very fist that had almost sent me into the next county. And then she screeched at me. Yes, screeched in a very loud and ugly tone, and to be honest about it, the screeching hurt me worse than the actual blow.

Well, maybe not. It was a heck of a punch, came all the way from the horse pasture, seemed to me, and it did cause my lights to blink there for a while.

But she screeched at me. "GET AWAY FROM MY BABY, YOU STINKING FLEABAG!!"

Boy, that hurt, it really did. Sometimes a dog wonders what it takes to please these people. I mean, you devote every waking hour to . . . oh well.

And then she screeched again, while I was trying my best to get out of her range. "Slim, either get this dog out of here or bring me the shotgun!"

Holy smokes, the mention of the shotgun cleared my head faster than smelling sauce, and even though I was still seeing sparklers and checkers and strange patterns of light behind my eyes, I took this opportunity to tuck my tail and scramble for safety under Slim's pickup.

I made it, and lucky for me, she didn't try to crawl under there to get me.

You know, I never did figger out what had lit her fuse. Baby Molly ended up eating the bug. Maybe that was it, but with these women, you never know.

Maybe I Stunk but Slim Got Bucked Off

So there I was, hiding under the pickup. Slim bent down and twisted his head so that our eyes met. I whapped my tail on the ground, as if to say, "I'm innocent, honest. All I did was ..."

He grinned. "Old Sally May packs a pretty mean right hand, don't she? Ha! Don't know as I ever saw her punch out a dog before. You've sure got a way with the ladies, pooch. Reminds me of me."

He hung the gas nozzle back on its baling-wire hook on the southwest angle-iron leg of the gas tanks. Then he climbed into the pickup and called out, "Come on, Stinkbomb. You ride in the back."

Riding in the back was fine with me, and it had nothing to do with me being a so-called

"Stinkbomb." Any ranch dog worth talking about will ride in the back of the pickup where the wind can blow his ears around and he can see what's going on in the world.

And just for the record, let me state that I didn't care for the way HE smelled either. At least I took a bath every day.

We turned right at the mailbox and drove to Slim's place, down the creek a mile or so from headquarters. He lived in that shack beneath the cottonwoods, the one that was covered with tarpaper because he and Loper had never gotten around to putting on the siding.

They hate any kind of work that involves a hammer. Let me rephrase that: They hate any kind of work that involves work, and I'm not saying that just because Slim had called me a so-called "Stinkbomb," although that did strike a sensitive nerve.

We puffed up to the front door, which faced the creek on the east, and he went inside. As he closed the screen door behind him, he turned back to me and said, "You stay out here, Rosebud."

Okay, that did it. I'd had it up to HERE with his name-calling and his cutting, cruel, childish remarks. By George, if he didn't like the way I smelled, he could just try to catch the rustlers without me.

You know what I did? I quit! Yes sir, right then and there, I walked off the job. I set my course in a southwesterly direction and said good-bye to a crummy job on a crummy third-rate ranch and...

"Come here, Hank! Scraps."

... and, what the heck, he wasn't such a bad guy after all, and the least I could do was give him another chance. I, uh, went back to the porch and patched up our friendship over a plate of last night's cold greasy potatoes.

Don't get me wrong. I'm no pushover. I won't always settle for cold greasy potatoes, but he'd caught me at the right moment and somebody had to walk that extra mile to keep the friendship alive. Fortunately, I didn't have to walk a whole mile.

So we made our peace, Slim and I. While I wolfed down the cold 'taters and licked the plate (that was a special favor to him, since I knew how much he hated washing dishes), while I cleaned up the dishes, he started putting together his camping gear.

There was quite a lot of it: a tent, his cowboy bedroll, a gas lantern, fishing gear, pots and pans, cans of food, a yellow slicker, an axe, and a full box of Twinkies.

When he had it all loaded on the back of the pickup, he drove down to the corral, poured some sweet feed into several feed bunks, and whistled to his horses. They came at a trot, but before they could eat, they had to go through their usual mealtime ritual of biting, squealing, and kicking each other.

Horses are such gluttons. Have we discussed horses? I don't like 'em. Not only do they fight over every flake of corn, but they will go out of their way to attack and harass an innocent dog.

I glared at them through the boards of the corral fence. If one of them had dared to come within range, I would have nipped him on the fetlocks. It's a procedure I've developed over the years—shooting my neck through the space between the two bottom boards and giving them a good stern bite before they know what's happening—and it DOES get their attention.

Yes, every now and then a guy gets kicked, but with these horses, you've got to take what you can get.

While the horses were eating and biting each other, Slim carried a packsaddle out of the shed and brushed the dust off of it. He haltered Jughead, the green colt, and tied the lead rope to a stout post. Then he started rigging him up with the packsaddle.

When he'd tightened the cinch, he stepped back

and said, "Well, that wasn't so bad. I'd thought we might see a little rodeo."

Then he started piling on the camping gear. When he'd gotten the load balanced, he covered it with a tarp and lashed it down, stepped back to admire his work and said, "Now ain't that a pretty load, Hank?"

I barked. It looked pretty good to me.

Then he threw a saddle on old Dunny, his favorite usin' horse, and we were ready to set out on a new adventure. Slim opened the corral gate and stepped up into the saddle. Holding Jughead's lead rope in his right hand, he nudged Dunny with the spurs and started toward the open gate.

Jughead didn't move. Slim tried several times to coax him into a walk, but the colt had decided that he didn't want to go camping, thank you. Slim pulled his hat down tight and said, "Okay, it looks like we'll have to go to Plan B. Stand by for action, Hank. This may get a little western."

I stood by for action.

He circled Dunny around and got some slack in the lead rope. Then he dallied the rope around the saddlehorn, took a deep breath, jabbed old Dunny with the spurs, and yelled, "Bite him, Hank!"

At that point things began to happen real fast. Jughead had pretty muchly made up his mind that he wasn't going to move, but when the slack went out of that lead rope, he got several surprises.

The first was that Dunny weighed 1,150 pounds, and when he got all those pounds moving in one direction, whatever was tied onto him was likely to move with him. The colt braced his legs, went back on the rope, fought like a tiger, and got jerked halfway across the corral.

The second surprise came when I shot under the bottom board of the fence and went on the attack. After I'd tattooed his hind legs several times with my teeth, he decided that leaving the barn might be a pretty good idea.

I love biting horses. I'd rather bite a horse than eat a bone, to tell you the truth.

Yes sir, we had our little parade moving in the right direction. Only trouble was that once we got Jughead moved off of high center, he went to pitching and tried to shuck that packsaddle off his back.

And once Jughead started bucking, Dunny must have thought that sounded like fun, 'cause he started bucking too, and all at once old Slim had his hands full of broncs.

I think one bronc would have been plenty. If he'd dropped Jughead's rope and concentrated on lining out Dunny, he'd have been prouder of his ride, but Slim was stubborn and hated to give slack to that smart-aleck colt, and he kept his dallies tight and tried to ride out the storm.

He did all right through the first five jumps, but halfway around the horse-pasture fence, he ran out of saddle glue. I knew what was coming when I saw him lose his left stirrup. The right stirrup was the next to go, followed a moment later by Slim himself.

When Dunny planted his front feet in the ground and dropped his head, Slim flew south, Dunny went west, and Jughead bucked off to the east.

The dust was so thick that I had to move around to get a better view. Through the cloud of dust, I saw old Slim dog-paddling over the top of Dunny's ears. After a short flight, he landed face-first in the middle of a clump of sagebrush.

At that point, I did what any loyal cowdog would do—rushed to the scene of the crash and administered an emergency Red Cross lick on the face. It must have worked. Slim sat up, grabbed a handful of dirt, and threw it in Jughead's direction.

My goodness, he looked a little mussed. One side of his face was covered with dust, while the other had taken on the color of fresh sagebrush. His glasses had come to rest on his upper lip and there was a new crease in his hat.

He sat there for a moment, staring at the toes of his boots, while I stared at his socks, which showed through the holes in the bottoms. He was wearing one white sock and one red sock, which I thought was kind of interesting.

"You know, I didn't think that dun horse could buck me off." He smiled, revealing a set of dirt-covered teeth. "But I'll bet he ain't horse enough to do it twice in one day." He picked himself up off the ground and moaned. "Say, that old dirt feels harder than it used to."

He limped over and caught Dunny's reins, tightened the cinch and swung aboard. "You old fool, you want to buck? Try that one more time and we'll see who's the champion on this ranch."

He leaned back in the saddle, slapped Dunny across the ears with his hat, raked him with the spurs, and squalled, "Go to it, son!"

Dunny snorted and went to work and . . . I'm sorry to report that Slim didn't quite make it to the whistle. I arrived on the scene just as the dust cloud was drifting away. Slim appeared to be hugging a sagebrush, and he had lost his hat.

I licked him on the ear. He raised his head and pushed me away. "Well, I told him to buck and he sure did. This time, I think I'll encourage him NOT to buck and see what happens. I'd hate for him to make a habit of that."

He caught the horse and talked to him for a minute, swung up into the saddle, loped him around the pasture in a figure eight, and warmed him up, which he probably should have done to start with.

Then he picked up the pack horse and we headed off to the north. The rodeo was over, and now we were riding off to a new adventure—catching rustlers in the canyon.

CHAPTER SIX

The Case of the Poisoned Weenies

~~~~~~

It was a beautiful day to be setting out on an adventure, with a nice breeze out of the southeast and a few puffy clouds floating along overhead.

We'd had some good spring rains, and the country north of Wolf Creek sure had its Sunday clothes on. The buffalo grass was tall and green, the beargrass had put out its white blooms, and the hills showed splashes of red, yellow, and purple where the wildflowers grew.

We didn't take the most direct route to the canyon pasture, and it took me a while to figger out why. Then I realized that Slim didn't want to leave any tracks on the main trail. So instead of entering the canyon from the south, we looped up north a

48

ways and came in from that direction, taking a narrow cow trail down to the bottom of the canyon.

Say, that was a wild and lonesome place. I'd done a little exploring of that canyon farther down, where the walls weren't quite as high and steep, but I'd never felt very comfortable about being there.

And for good reason. Those canyons were famous for growing the biggest, meanest, hungriest coyotes in Ochiltree County, and on our way down the canyon rim, I found it convenient to, shall we say, keep very little distance between me and the horses.

Don't get me wrong. I'm no chicken liver, but I'd had enough experience with those wild coyote warriors to know that they could sure mess up a dog's camping trip.

It was along about five in the evening when we reached the spot where Slim wanted to make camp. It was near the head of the canyon, close to a spring-fed pool of water, and with enough old dead wood around to feed a campfire.

He hobbled the horses in a grassy flat and pitched his little two-man pup tent . . . or was it a two-pup man tent? One or the other, I can't remember, but it was just about the right size for two men or two pups or one man and one pup.

Anyways, he pitched the tent, rolled out my bed (I didn't know where HE planned to sleep, but I staked my claim on that bedroll right away), got a fire going in the fire pit, and made a pot of coffee.

By this time the sun had dropped behind the west rim of the canyon and the shadows were getting long. He brought out his cast-iron skillet and started supper. He cooked up some bacon and used the grease to fry some potatoes and weenies.

That was his supper: bacon, fried potatoes, and weenies. I watched him eat, and he even pitched me a bite or two, but to tell you the truth, I've never been crazy about weenies.

Oh, they taste all right at first, but after you eat a couple of 'em, what you begin to notice is the garlic. Me and garlic don't get along. So it didn't bother me at all that Slim ate most of the burned weenies himself, and by then it was getting dark and he went to work cleaning up the supper mess and . . .

Hmm, he had left the open package of weenies sitting there on a rock. I wondered if he had left them there for a reason or if . . .

Slim wasn't what you'd call a careless person. Okay, maybe he WAS a careless person but not so careless that he would leave an open package of weenies sitting on a rock without a reason.

What could this mean? I watched him as he wiped out his skillet and put things away and began fiddling with his gas lantern. He showed no interest whatsoever in the package of weenies.

Hmmmmm.

At last I narrowed the range of explanations down to two. Explanation One: He had left the weenies out on purpose and was conducting a test of my willpower. Explanation Two: He had left them out on purpose, knowing that I had worked up an appetite and that dogs must eat.

Okay, the next step was to devise a clever test that would narrow the range of possibilities down to one. I scooted myself closer to the alleged weenies and gave them a good sniffing, and, by George, they smelled pretty good, but the point of the experiment was to see if Slim would snatch them away and say, "Oh no you don't, pooch!"

He said nothing of the kind. In fact, he said nothing. He didn't notice. Or to frame it up more in line with the experiment, he had almost certainly put them there hoping that I would help myself.

That made sense. I mean, he was a busy guy. I had no right to expect him to stop what he was doing and feed me every bite of supper.

I gave the weenies another sniffing. Holy

smokes, those things smelled WONDERFUL! I love weenies, always have. Give me a choice between a package of raw weenies and a package of raw steak and I'll take weenies every time, especially if there's no package of steak around.

What's a little garlic? Garlic is actually very good for the digestion and some people even think it can cure a cold. I didn't have a cold but a guy never knows . . .

I, uh, scootched a little closer to the . . . and gave Slim one last careful observation, just to make sure that this wasn't one of his famous pranks. With these cowboys, you never want to take too much for granite. As I've said before, that's what tombstones are made of.

No, he was totally absorbed in his project of trying to light the lantern, which appeared to be giving him some trouble. Okay, there was my answer. I had submitted this deal to rigorous scientific testing and . . . what was I waiting for?

And so it was that, after completing the testing procedure and arriving at the only possible conclusion—that Slim wanted me to help myself to the weenies so that he could continue working on the lantern—after completing all the aforementioned so-forth, I, uh, eased my nose into the package of . . .

Just one. That's all I wanted. Just a taste, a little snack to tide me over until . . .

OH WONDERFUL WEENIE!

Boy, I hadn't realized just how hungry I was until I gobbled down that luscious weenie, and suddenly I realized just how hungry I was, and how much I loved fresh weenies and . . .

Maybe just one more.

He'd never miss two weenies out of a whole package. How many were in a package? Twelve? Twenty-four? A hundred and thirty-five?

Who'd miss two little weenies out of a huge package of 135? A normal man couldn't possibly eat 135 weenies on one camping trip—and shouldn't. He needed more variety in his diet, more vegetables and fruits and your other food groups.

Just one more.

Broccoli, that's what Slim needed in his diet, lots of broccoli and cabbage and . . . gulp, slurp . . . you know, the great thing about weenies is that . . . slurp, gulp . . . they don't require a whole lot of . . . gulp, slurp . . . chewing. And they also taste . . . slurp, gulp, slurp . . . delicious.

Yes, Slim definitely needed more . . . slurp, gulp . . . broccoli in his . . .

One weenie left?

You know, once a guy has committed himself to a certain course of action—and we're talking about actions that could lead to serious consequences—once a guy has charted his course, so to speak, it's not a bad idea to eat the map.

That sounds odd, doesn't it, so let's go straight to the point. We're talking about evidence. One weenie left in a package can be interpreted as evidence, whereas no weenies and no package can be interpreted as an honest mistake.

Someone "misplaced" the package of weenies. Forgot to put it in its proper place. It just disappeared. It happens all the time.

So, to avoid even the appearance of wrongdoing, which could cause friction among the, uh, campers, I chose to . . . that is, the last weenie vanished. And so did the empty package. Leaving not a trace behind.

Burp.

Boy, I had definitely caught my limit of weenies for one night, and I wouldn't have minded giving two or three of 'em back, to tell you the truth.

Darkness had fallen and Slim had finally gotten his lantern going, and he looked very proud of himself as he . . . burp. You ever eat so many weenies at one sitting that you could hardly walk?

Anyway, Slim looked very proud of himself, and he stood up and yawned and . . .

You ever wonder how it would feel to fall into a huge vat of garlic juice? Garlic everywhere! You can smell it, taste it, hear it, feel it, see it.

The only trouble with burp weenies is that they can turn on you. Once they reach your stomach, they begin releasing a deadly burp, excuse me, garlic toxin, which is why I've always hated stupid weenies, and why I quit eating them the last time I burp ate them.

And if I never see another weenie again in my whole life, that'll be okay with me.

Slim looked off to the southwest where lightning was twinkling in the distance. "Looks like Amarillo's getting a shower. This grass could use one but I'd just as soon it waited a week." He yawned. "Well, pup, I don't know about you but I've had about all the fun I can stand for one day. Let's turn in. Who knows, we may be up with cow thieves tonight."

He pulled off his boots and jeans, turned off the lantern, and crawled into the tent. I staggered in behind him, curled up beside his head, and hoped that death would come sooner rather than later.

Burp.

Never, ever, EVER would I touch another stupid . . .

Slim sat straight up in bed. Maybe he'd heard the rustlers coming. I didn't care. As far as I was concerned, they could take the whole ranch.

"I smell . . . garlic."

Oh yeah? Big deal. I was embalmed with garlic.

"I wonder if I put those weenies . . ." There was a long throbbing moment of silence. "Hank, you hammerhead, you ate all my camp meat, didn't you!"

Yes, I did it, I confess. Go ahead and shoot me, you'll be doing me a big favor.

He kicked me out of the tent. That was okay. I'd always wanted to die outside under the burp.

Stars. I hate weenies.

Slim Gets Soaked Because of a Faulty Tent Rope

We needn't go into gory details. I had become one sick puppy and I didn't care where I slept that night, because I didn't suppose that I would be sleeping anyway.

Who can sleep in a garlic factory?

But nature has provided us with a way of curing such problems—two ways, actually. The first is called "Death by Poisoning." The second is called "Reverse Peristroika." I would have settled for either one, but it happened that peristroika took hold of my entire digestive system and turned it wrongside-out in the space of just a few minutes.

Slim had made a real smart move when he

threw me out of the tent. Fellers, if I'd stayed in there for another three minutes, we might have been forced to burn the tent and all our bedding.

Well, nature took its course and I escaped death-by-garlic by the narrowest of margins, and right then and there I placed "camp meat" on the list of Toxic Products Not Even Fit for Hogs. Me and weenies had just declared war on each other, is what had happened.

I had acquired a new and passionate hatred for ... although I must admit that once I had cleared out the plumbing, so to speak, the thought did occur to me ...

No. Absolutely no more weenies.

After taking the Anti-Weenie Pledge and conducting a thorough purge of all systems, I turned to the task of putting my life back together. I had lost my right to sleep in the tent, which was okay because your higher breeds of dogs ...

Coyotes howling?

A restless wind moaning in the trees?

Flashes of lightning that seemed to be coming closer?

I've never been the kind of dog who gets spooked by coyotes howling in the distance. The key word there is DISTANCE. We figger that 2–3 miles is a comfortable margin, but the howling I had begun to pick up appeared to be quite a bit closer than that, and coming closer all the time. You ever notice that a dying campfire throws eerie shadows on the side of a tent? Yes sir, and not only are they eerie, but they also MOVE AROUND. I watched those shadows for a while and . . . by George, they began to look a whole lot like cattle rustlers.

Three horrible-looking villains slouched through camp with guns and knives. One of 'em had three eyes. Another had two heads. The third one had the tail of a lizard and I didn't suppose that Slim would notice if I crept back inside the . . .

"Get out of here, you weenie thief! I don't need you burping garlic in my face all night. Scram."

Actually, the garlic had . . . but yes, he seemed pretty emphatic about booting me out of house and home, and let me say right here that I've never been the kind of dog who has a pathagorical fear of thunder and lightning.

Some dogs do, you know, and I happen to work with one: Drover. Drover is scared of storms. Oh, he might bark at the first thumber of rundle and the first flash of lightning, but after that, you won't find him again until the next day. He runs for the machine shed and hides until the storm passes over.

Me? I'm the kind of dog who stands his ground,

faces the thunder and lightning, and the lightning and thunder were coming closer and closer, and with the coyotes howling and those shadows swooping around on the side of the tent . . .

I wouldn't say that I was scared. *Concerned* would be closer to it. Nervous. Why else would a normal dog start chewing on the tent rope? It was just a simple case of nerves, that's all.

I mean, when a guy gets nervous, he's got to do something, right? I'll admit that it wasn't my best idea of the year, but at the time it seemed . . . it made me feel better about things, that's all, as I watched that huge cloud advancing toward us.

Suddenly the wind shifted and carried the smell of dampness, and I could hear the roar of the rain coming up the canyon, and then IT HIT US.

Wind? My goodness, what a wind. And rain? Buckets of rain, sheets of rain, so much rain that I could hardly breathe, and . . . somehow the, uh, tent rope snapped (cheap material) and the tent collapsed in a heap. And then . . .

You won't believe this. I could hardly believe it myself, but here goes. That tent suddenly *turned into a ghost!* Honest, no kidding. I saw it with my own eyes in the eerie silver glow of the lightning. That thing sat up, moved its arms, and started yelling!

Well, you know me. A ghost can get me worked
up in a hurry, and that thing caused a strip of hair
to raise on my back, all the way from my ears back
to the base of my tailbone, and fellers, I BARKED.

Yes sir, I barked at that awful thing in the wind
and the rain, trying my best to alert Slim to . . .

Speaking of Slim, where was he? He must have
disappeared when . . .

Okay, I think we've worked this thing out.

False alarm. Let's move along with the story, and you can forget the business about the ghost. It turned out to be a simple case of mistaken identity. No problem.

Next day.

We had a rather cold, wet, and miserable night, one reason being that in his haste to set up camp the previous afternoon, Slim had used an inferior grade of rope on the tent. In the light of the next morning, it appeared that one of the main ropes had actually snapped under the strain of the wind and rain, causing the tent to collapse.

The very worst time for a tent to collapse is in the midst of a rainstorm. A collapsed tent suddenly loses its ability to shed water, don't you see, and . . . it was quite a mess that greeted us by the dawn's early light.

Slim had gotten very little sleep during the night. His eyes were red and puffy, and he was in a terrible humor. As he hung the bedding and his clothes on cedar trees to dry, he kept coming back to that treacherous tent rope. He held the two frayed ends in his hands and studied them.

"I can't believe the stupid tent rope busted, just when I needed it most. You don't need a fool tent until it rains, and then when it rains, the dadgum thing falls apart!"

I sat there beside him, thumping my tail on the ground and sharing his sense of outrage at the inferior quality of modern tents. Somebody should have been sued for this. There was absolutely no excuse for it.

By George, if they were going to be in the tent business, they ought to build a tent that could stand up to the elements of nature. And if they couldn't do that, then they ought to find another line of work.

I was outraged. Slim was outraged. We were both just about as outraged as we could be. Why, Slim was so worked up that he vowed to write a letter to the president of the tent company. I didn't blame him. I would have done the same thing except that dogs don't write letters.

Well, our camp was a pretty dull place for the rest of the day. Whilst everything was hanging up to dry, Slim curled up in the shade of a cedar bush and tried to catch up on all the sleep he'd missed during the night.

That left me with the job of guarding camp against rustlers and wild prowling animals, which I did with all my heart and soul and . . . zzzzzzzzzz.

I did manage to catch a few winks of sleep somewhere in the middle of the afternoon. Not much, just a quick nap, and only when I was certain that our camp would be safe.

Short nap, very short, certainly not enough to be considered a breach of security.

By evening, things had returned to normal. The stuff had dried out and Slim had raised the tent again, but this time he replaced the inferior tent rope with his nylon pigging string.

He was in a better mood now—although he continued to make a big issue out of the "camp meat" that I had . . . the camp meat that had mysteriously vanished the night before.

He blamed me for it, but that was okay. I had broad soldiers. I could take it. Shoulders, I should say, broad shoulders.

He boiled some coffee and fried up some bacon and beans, and by the time darkness fell over our little outpost, he was feeling pretty good—so good, in fact, that he offered to sing me a song around the campfire.

What could I say? I didn't happen to be a major fan of his singing, but nobody pays a dog for his opinions, so I listened.

Here's how it went:

Alas and Alack

'Twas the Fourth of July when I read in
    the paper

That a circus from Kansas had pulled into town.
Now elephants had always kind of intrigued me
And I hadn't seen a woman in a month and a
    half.

A feller gets crazy in bachelor quarters,
And wishes to gaze on a woman or two.
And so I forsook all the boss's fine Herefords
And went to the circus, alas and alack.

At two hundred yards I thought she was
    gorgeous,
She looked like a mermaid with long golden
    hair.
Somehow I missed the tattoo on her shoulder
And that she weighed in close to three
    hundred pounds.

I should have looked closer before I embraced
    her,
It never occurred to me that she might have
The hairiest armpits in Ochiltree County.
I really goofed up there, alas and alack!

I guess that some lassies ain't wild about
    cowboys

Who sneak up and grab 'em and kiss on
   their face.
In any event, though, she screamed like a
   panther
And messed up my jaw with a wicked left
   hook.

I sure 'nuff was shocked that she had that big
   husband,
A wrestler, in fact, with a bone in his nose.
Before he got finished, I really looked forward
To seeing my Herefords, alas and alack.

I'm warning you boys who stay on them
   ranches,
A circus is dangerous to fellers like us.
There's something about all those glittering
   costumes
That makes a poor cowboy go out of his mind.

Beware of the women with big hairy husbands,
Especially the ones with a bone in their nose.
In courting a lass, a lack of good judgment
Can shorten your lifespan, alas and alack!

CHAPTER EIGHT

The Mysterious Visitor in the Night

In many ways Slim is a fine guy, but a great singer he will never be.

By the time he'd finished the song, darkness had fallen across the canyon and we found ourselves looking up at the black velvet sky, sprayed with thousands of glittering stars.

Slim pointed to the sky and said, "Well, Hank, there's the Big Dipper."

Oh really? I studied the sky for a long time and saw nothing but stars.

"And there's O'Brien the Hunter."

Okay, some big guy named O'Brien was up there hunting and dipping snuff, and just in case he decided to spit, I moved my business into the tent. It was past my bedtime anyway.

I spent a minute or two digging around on the bedroll, until I had created a spot that was soft enough to hold my freight for the night, and then I collapsed.

It felt wonderful and I fell right off to sleep, and would have stayed asleep through the entire night if Slim hadn't come blundering into the tent and started accusing me of "hogging" his bedroll.

Hey, who'd gotten there first? Who'd taken the time to dig it up and fluff it up and warm it up? ME. But never mind property law, never mind what was good and right. He bullied his way onto the bedroll and managed to push me off onto the cold hard ground.

I didn't sleep well on the cold hard ground, and before long I began hearing strange noises coming from Slim's side of the tent. I sat up and listened. Slim had mentioned something about "hogging." Now I was hearing sounds that almost surely were coming from hogs. Was there a pattern here?

My goodness, did we have HOGS in the tent with us? Yes, by George, someone or something had turned a bunch of hogs loose inside our tent!

Well, you know me. I'm not the kind of dog who'll turn over and go to sleep while a herd of wild boars is running loose in the tent, so I did what any Head of Ranch Security would have done: I barked. Boy howdy, did I bark!

Suddenly the oinking stopped. Slim sat up in bed. "Hank, shut up. It's just me snoring."

Oh.

"And if you can't handle that, go sleep outside."

No, that was fine, no problem. I'd just thought . . . hey, I'd never heard sounds like that coming from a human, I mean, we're talking about real heavy-duty pig noises.

"Now go to sleep."

Okay, fine. You never know until you check these things out. I'd done my job and checked it out and . . . boy, that guy made an incredible amount of noise in his sleep. Beat anything I'd ever heard before.

I waited until he started snoring again and then I slipped back and reclaimed my spot on the bedroll. That was much better than the cold hard ground, although I had a little trouble drifting off because his nose kept poking me in the ribs.

I don't know how long I'd been asleep, but sometime in the middle of the night my ears shot up. I lifted my head and waited for my eyes to stop rolling around.

Unless I was badly mistaken, I'd heard a sound in the distance, and this time it wasn't Slim's snoring. No, it sounded more like . . . holy smokes, it sounded like the hum of a pickup motor and the rattling of a stock trailer!

A growl began to form in my throat, then I leaped to my feet and began to bark. Suddenly and out of nowhere, a foot appeared out of nowhere and booted me out of the tent!

"Dadgum barking dog, get out of here!"

Oh, that must have been Slim's foot and he had . . . but obviously he hadn't heard what I had heard, and what I had heard just might be a *gang of cattle rustlers coming into the pasture.*

I mean, that's why we were camping out in the pasture, right? And it was my job to sound the alarm when I heard strange noises out there in the pasture, right? Okay, that was my job and I had every intention of . . .

SPLAT!

He had just clubbed me with a pillow. Can you believe it? There I was, trying to fulfill the mission that had been assigned to me and . . .

"Dry up, Hank!"

Okay, fine. I could dry up. I could let him sleep his life away, if that's what he wanted, and I could let the rustlers carry off all of Uncle Johnny's calf crop too.

What did I care? I hadn't asked for a combat

71

assignment. I would have been perfectly happy to stay back at headquarters. Did he think that camping out on the hard ground and listening to him snore and eating poisoned weenies was my idea of fun?

Hey, he wanted me to dry up? Fine. He wanted to sleep? Terrific. I could sleep too. I didn't have to take all his screeching and kicking. I got paid the same whether I caught cattle rustlers or not, so phooey on him and his lousy . . .

But you know what? I tried to sleep but I couldn't. I tried not to care but I did. I guess that's one of the marks of a true top-of-the-line blue-ribbon cowdog: we care about things, even when nobody else does, even when there seems to be no reason to care.

Your ordinary dog would have turned over and gone back to sleep, but my ma didn't raise me to be ordinary. It appeared that I would have to tackle this thing alone, solve the entire case without the help of anyone else, and before I could ponder the consequences of such a bold decision, I left camp in a run and headed out into the deep darkness of the canyon.

If I had stopped to ponder this deal, one of the things I might have pondered about was that I would be traveling alone through a canyon that was known to be infested with cannibals.

That would have been dangerous enough in the light of day, when most cannibals are asleep in their holes, but traveling at night . . .

Gulp. My bold decision was looking worse all the time. I mean, there's a fine line between bravery and really stupid behavior.

Well, there was nothing to do but mush on and hope for the best.

We had made our camp near the north end of the pasture and the rustlers, if that's who they were, would be coming through the south gate, about a mile away. How did I know that? Simple, That pasture was so rough, there was only one road in and and one road out.

I must have run a good half-mile when I stopped on a high bluff to catch my breath and reconnoiter the country ahead. Looking south down the canyon, I could see . . . holy cats, the flash of headlights!

Sure enough, *somebody was driving around in the pasture.* Not only did that give me a creepy feeling, but it proved that I was wearing a very sensitive and high-quality set of ears. I had suspected all along that they were pretty good ears, and this was sure 'nuff proof of it.

Picked up the sound of a stock trailer rattling a whole mile away. Pretty good ears.

And that led naturally into the next question, which I posed aloud to myself. "Okay, Hankie Boy, we've got this investigation going in the right direction. What do we do now?"

I was surprised—nay, shocked, astounded, and stupified—when a voice other than my own responded to that question. The voice said, "You know, I've been sitting here, axing myself that very same question."

My mouth suddenly went dry. Was I dreaming this mystery voice in the night? No, I was wide awake. Did that voice belong to Slim? No way. Was there any other voice that I might want to hear in the middle of a pasture in the middle of the night? Absolutely not.

Hence, I reached for the afterburners and . . . WHAM . . . ran into something big, hairy, and immovable—something so big that even the force of my afterburners didn't make an impression on it. And fellers, that was BIG.

I was in the process of picking myself off the ground and trying to restart my breathing mechanisms, when I heard the thing say, "Oops, sorry. I didn't see you there."

Oops? Hadn't I met someone in recent days who had used that expression? I ran that through my data banks, calling up a search using "Oops" as the key word. The massive mainframe that resides between my ears clicked and whirred, and within seconds it spit out a single name.

"Brewster? Is that you? Please say yes, because if you say no, it will mean that I just ran over a cannibal in the darkness."

"Yeah, it was me all right, and I'm no camel. Just a dog."

"Great, oh boy, that's a relief, but I said cannibal, not camel."

"Oh. I wondered. Never saw a camel around here."

"There's a reason for that, Brewster. We have no camels on this ranch, but unfortunately this pasture is crawling with cannibals."

"Aw heck. What does a cammibal look like?"

"They look like coyotes, they're always hungry, and they will eat a ranch dog if given the slightest opportunity. But never mind that. What in the name of thunderation are you doing out here in the middle of the night?"

He yawned. "You know, that's a long story, and I just don't know whether I have the energy to tell it or not."

"Make the energy, Brewster, and tell it. It could be very important to this case."

And with that, I began the long and tedious process of interrogating Brewster the Dog, which proved to be a long and tedious process, but one which yielded some very important information—such as . . .

Well, you'll see. Just keep reading.

YIKES!

Little by little, piece by piece, yawn by yawn, I dragged the story out of the huge sleepy-eyed German shepherd–St. Bernard crossbred dog before me.

First, Uncle Johnny was a restless little cuss who couldn't sleep when he thought rustlers might be stealing his cattle.

Second, he had wanted to see if he could penetrate Slim's and my early-warning defense systems.

Third, Uncle Johnny had thought that he could drive through the pasture without headlights. Fourth, Uncle Johnny had sure been wrong about that, because, fifth, he had driven his pickup into a ravine, and sixth, he was now stuck somewhere in the pasture.

Pacing back and forth in front of Brewster, I made careful notes and entered all the data. "All right, Brewster, I have a few more questions and then we'll have this thing wrapped up. Were you guys pulling a stock trailer?"

"Let's see. Stock trailer."

"One that rattled?"

"One that rattled. Hmmm."

I waited. "A simple yes or no will do."

"Well, let me think here. I was taking a little nap, see."

"Are you saying that you don't know whether you were pulling a stock trailer or not?"

"No, I didn't want to come right out and say that."

"But is it true?"

"It'ud make me sound a little neglectful, wouldn't it?"

"Yes, Brewster, I'm afraid it would."

"Then if it's all the same to you, I'd just as soon not . . ." His statement trailed off into a big yawn. "Boy, I'm not used to these late nights."

I stopped pacing and went nose-to-nose with him. In the darkness, I had the feeling that I was facing the head of a stuffed moose.

"Brewster, I must know the answer. On the night of . . . well, tonight . . . were you or were you not pulling a stock trailer?"

"Well, I wasn't. Not me myself. See, it's not my pickup, although I sleep in it quite a bit of the time."

I heaved a sigh and walked a short distance away. "Brewster, you're a very large dog and I would never accuse a large dog of being stupid, but sometimes your answers border on being stupid. I must know if Uncle Johnny was pulling a stock trailer tonight when he entered this pasture."

"Okay, let me think here." I could hear him yawning. I was close to becoming annoyed with his yawning, but then he spoke. "No, I don't think we were pulling a trailer."

"Great! Thanks for a straight answer." I began pacing again. "All right, next question. Brewster, what are you doing here?"

"Well, let's see." Long pause. "Boy, that's a good question."

"Thanks. Do you have a good answer?"

"Nope, not really. It's kindly peculiar, ain't it?"

"Yes, Brewster, it is. Try to reconstruct the sequence of events. Where were you when Uncle Johnny drove into the ravine?"

"Uh . . . boy, that's a toughie. Knowing me, I was probably in the back, asleep."

"You sleep a lot, don't you, Brewster?"

"Yeah," he yawned, "it takes a lot of sleep to keep this old body running in top shape."

"So you were asleep in the back of the pickup. What happened then?"

"I guess I woke up. Yeah, I did. It was quite a shock."

"So how did you get from there to here?"

"You just keep firing those questions, don't you?"

"Firing questions is my job, Brewster. I'm Head of Ranch Security. How did you get from there to here?"

"Well..." Long silence, punctured now and then by big yawns. "Okay, Uncle Johnny cussed himself for driving off in a hole. Then I heard him say that he was too old to walk all the way down to Loper's place. Then... you know, you're going to wear me out with all this talking."

"Just a little more, Brewster, and then we'll be done."

"Oh boy." Yawn. "I guess the next thing was that he told me to go find y'all's camp."

"And?"

"Uhhhhhh... I guess I didn't find it. I'd just laid down to catch a few winks when you came along. That was pretty lucky."

I chuckled. "Not luck, Brewster. In this business

81

we call it 'Brute Skill.' You see, I had a suspicion that I'd find you out here, and sure enough, I did it, traveling strictly on instruments."

He yawned. "My instruments don't work that good."

"Because they're always asleep, Brewster. Nobody's instruments work when they're asleep. You need to work on staying awake."

"Yeah, right. Speaking of which, do we have time for a little nap? These late hours are killing me."

"I'm afraid not, for you see, Brewster, while I was looking for you, I picked up the telltale sounds of a stock trailer rattling around in this pasture, and if that reading was correct, then it can mean only one thing."

Zzzzzzzzzzzzzz.

"Brewster?" He had fallen asleep. "All right, you big lug, you want to sleep, so sleep. I'm leaving and you can find your own way out of here. I have work to do and I didn't want you tagging along anyway. Is that clear?"

Zzzzzzzzzzzzzz.

"Fine. Good-bye, and I hope you get bedsores."

And with that, I left Brewster where he lay and went on about my business, solving the Case of the Midnight Rustlers.

I struck out across country, heading in a southwesterly direction toward the glow of the phantom headlights. Yes, they were still in the pasture, working their crinimal mischief, and they would soon learn some bitter lessons about stealing cattle in MY part of the world.

At last I reached the last bluff between me and the lights. I slowed to a walk and then to a crawl. I lowered my body to ground level and began inching my way to the top of the hill. And suddenly I was there, looking down at the scene before me.

A single figure dressed in cowboy clothes was walking in the beam of the headlights. He was carrying a partially filled sack of cattle feed and scattering it out on the ground. And he was calling the cattle in to feed: "Woooooo, cow! Wooooo, darlings!"

And did I mention the portable corral panels? That was pretty slick. See, he had rigged up some racks on both sides of his stock trailer so that he could carry enough portable corral panels to build a small pen. He had already set up three sides of the pen and he was scattering the feed so as to lure the cattle inside.

Yes, I had his MO down now. Once he had drawn a little bunch of cattle inside, he would slip out and close the circle with the rest of the panels.

Oh, this guy was clever! I had to give him credit for that, and also for his understanding of livestock. You can tell, just by the way a man moves and carries himself, whether or not he's accustomed to working around cattle. If that guy had made any sudden moves or loud noises, the cattle would have scattered to the four corners of the pasture.

But his manner was smooth and quiet, and derned if the cattle weren't coming in to feed. I wouldn't have bet he could do that. I mean, cattle are pretty stupid but they're naturally suspicious of a stranger who shows up in their pasture in the middle of the night.

It made me suspect that this creep had been coming over here for months, feeding little bunches at night to get them used to his routine. Cattle are suckers for a routine, don't you know, especially when it involves free food.

Well, I had seen enough to wrap this case up. It was time to swoop down and . . . someone was standing beside me—Brewster, no doubt, who had finally dragged himself out of the vapors of sleep and decided to make a hand.

"Well, it's about time you got here. I thought I was going to have to . . ."

Brewster didn't have yellow eyes, did he? Or a sharp-pointed nose? And if this was Brewster, how come I was seeing double all at once?

I, uh, glanced from one set of eyes to the other. "Brewster, if this is your idea of a joke, I'm not amused."

And then a voice replied, "Not rooster, and not joke. Only Rip and Snort, ho ho!"

YIKES!

CHAPTER TEN

The Last Crusade

Well, I had known all along that the canyon pasture was crawling with coyotes, and here they were, about to crawl all over me.

Actually, I wasn't too worried about it. If they appeared to be in a hostile frame of mind, all I had to do to escape their clutches was trot down the hill and join up with the cattle rustler. It's a well-known fact that coyotes won't go near a human, whereas a dog . . . well, you get the picture.

Yes, the idea of joining forces with a cow thief raised a few ethical problems, but hungry cannibals have a way of ironing out a lot of ethical problems.

In other words, what faced me now wasn't actually a matter of life and death but a minor inconvenience that might delay my wrapping up the case. With that in mind, I greeted their snarling faces with an air of easy self-confidence.

"Well, by George, look what the cats dragged up!"

"That you, Hunk? Same Hunk-dog we see before many time?"

"I admit it. Yes, I'm the same charming rascal who steals the hearts of the women and can out-sing you fleabags on any given day of any given week."

"Ha! Same Hunk-dog with big mouth and big stupid in head. Hunk in big trouble now 'cause coyote catch big-mouth stupidhead Hunk out in pasture, ha!"

I chuckled to myself "Hey guys, I hate to tell you this, but I'm not even a little bit scared. Do I look scared?"

They studied me with narrowed eyes. "Not looking scared. Looking stupid, away from house and boom-boom."

"Yes, but the point is that I don't look scared because I'm not scared, and I'm not scared because I know something you don't know. And because you don't know it, Snort, it follows from simple logic that YOU are scared."

They got a big laugh out of that. "Hunk talk

stupider and stupidest all time! Coyote not scared of nothing. Love to fight and sing rowdy song and beat up whole world, oh boy, and maybe eat Hunk for breakfast too."

I joined in with their laughter. "Yes, but you're forgetting one small detail, Snort. Knowledge is power. If I know something you don't know, then I am stronger than you. And if I'm stronger than you, there's nothing you can do to me, right?"

This got their attention. It had taken a while but the truth had finally dripped through the coffeemaker of their minds.

"What Hunk know that coyote not know?"

"Well, if I told you, then you would know and I'd lose my power."

"Uh. But if Hunk not tell, coyote not believe and maybe eat Hunk anyway."

Hmmm. I hadn't thought of that. He had a point there.

"Okay, I'll tell you, but you must solemnly swear never to use it against me because, well, that would be cheating. Can you do that?"

"Ha, coyote good for cheating."

"No, I mean solemnly swearing."

"Uh. Coyote not so good for sommenly swear."

"But you must solemnly swear or I won't tell

you. You have to take the whole deal or nothing at all."

They went into a huddle and whispered back and forth. Then Snort broke the circle and said, "Coyote have big conference, decide to take sommenly swear with whole deal."

"All right, raise your left paws."

Snort shook his head. "Not pause. Go right into whole deal with sommenly swear."

"No, no, you missed my point!"

"Not point at coyote. Coyote not like pointing-at-to-be."

I took a deep breath and studied the stars overhead. "Snort, let's back up and start over."

"Coyote not back up from nothing. Fight badger and bobcat, beat up skunk, play catch with rattlesnake, oh boy. Not back up from Hunk too."

"Okay, okay. Both of you, raise your left front foot." This threw them into confusion as they lifted first one foot and then the other.

"Got two front foots left."

"Yes, but only one left front foot. You see, all of us have a left foot and a right foot. To solemnly swear something, you're supposed to raise your right front paw. But I know you guys don't know left from right or right from wrong, so I told you to raise the left one—which is wrong—knowing that you would raise the wrong one instead, which of course is the right one."

Their small greenish eyes stared at me. "Right foot wrong?"

"No, the right foot is right, but I knew you'd make the wrong choice, so that would make the left foot right."

"Right foot left?"

"If you raised your right foot, your left foot would be left on the ground, that's right."

Snort clubbed me over the head with his right foot. "Hunk shut stupid mouth about foot and get on with sommenly swear."

"Okay, fine, sorry I mentioned it. Repeat after me: I, Snort the Coyote, do solemnly swear for myself and for my brother Rip, who never seems to talk, that we will not use Hank's secret information against him."

Four empty yellow eyes stared at me. "Too much for remember."

"Okay, just say, 'We do.'"

"You do."

"Not 'you do,' you dodo. WE DO."

He clubbed me over the head again. "Not call coyote a weed-dew!"

"I didn't call you a weed-dew. I called you a dodo."

"Uh. Dodo better than weed-dew. Coyote not like weed, and dew make everybody wet. Coyote not like wet."

"Great. Do we have a deal or not?"

"Uh. Got deal, good deal."

"In other words, you both solemnly swear?"

They nodded their heads. "Both sommenly swear."

Whew! Boy, I wasn't sure I'd ever get them sworn in. Our system of laws and orders sure wasn't designed for cannibals.

"Now Hunk tell secret knowledge, and pretty quick too."

"All right, here's the deal." Smiling to myself, I brought my mouth closer to their ears and whispered, "I know that you guys can't do any damage to me, because there's a man on the other side of this hill, see, and all I have to do is . . ."

The sneaking, scheming, counterfeit, two-timing, double-crossing, two-faced, cheating . . . you know what they did? In an instant, and I mean in the blink of an eye, they broke their solemn oaths, used my secret information against me, swapped ends, and placed their hulking bodies between me and my escape route.

I couldn't believe my own eyes. I was stunned. Shocked. Dismayed. Crushed. Disillusioned.

Also mad at myself for being stupid enough to trust them, what a dumb trick, how could I have been so brick-headed!

And now, blocking my escape route, they greeted me with huge fangs and glittering eyes. "Hey, you can't do this. You promised, you swore a solemn oath!"

"Ha! Coyote not give a hoot for sommenly oath. Coyote berry good to cheat, too bad for Hunk."

"Yes, but you probably didn't realize that once you've committed yourself to cheating, everybody in the world will call you a CHEATER. Is that how you want to live your life, Snort, with everybody in the whole world pointing at you and saying, 'Oh look at him, he's nothing but a cheater?'"

"Coyote not give a hoot for whole world pointing. Coyote not give a hoot for nothing but eat."

"Well, uh, gulp, maybe what you should do right now is, uh, sing your famous song about not giving a hoot. Wouldn't that be fun?"

They shook their heads. "Not fun. Only want eat Hunk for supper, oh boy."

Oh boy indeed. I couldn't even interest them in singing. That was a real bad sign. Another bad sign was that they began creeping toward me, grinning at me with wild crazy grins and licking their respective chops.

"No, wait, maybe we could . . . hey, I've got a great idea. Maybe instead of eating, we could . . ." They kept coming. "Weenies, that's what you guys need—a whole package of juicy weenies, where could we find some . . . don't look at me that way, Snort, it makes me . . ."

Nothing was working this time. I had talked my way out of this same situation several times in the past, but now . . . holy smokes, they kept creeping toward me! If I ran, they would follow me out into darkness of the pasture, but if I didn't run . . .

Fellers, all at once things were looking pretty bleak. There I was, a poor helpless ranch dog, standing in the middle of a big pasture, in the middle of the night and surrounded by hungry ferocious coyotes who had lied and cheated and tricked me and used my own natural honesty against me.

I would really hate to end it all right here, and I mean not only the story but also my entire career, but things had sure 'nuff gotten out of control for me and . . .

Anyways, they ate me and that's all the story. Sorry to disappoint you.

Good-bye.

Okay, Maybe
I Exaggerated, but
Not Much

I already told you that I was eaten alive by cannibals, so how come you kept on reading?

Maybe you just couldn't bring yourself to accept the awful truth. Maybe you couldn't bear the thought of facing life without a Head of Ranch Security.

Or maybe—this one is a very remote possibility but I'll mention it anyway—maybe you had a sneaking suspicion that I might have stretched the truth just a tad, and that maybe the cannibals didn't eat me after all. Or at least not all of me.

In other words, maybe they left just enough of me to continue the story.

Well, shame on you for having such thoughts, but that's kind of what happened, actually. They didn't get me entirely eaten, see, and left just exactly enough of me to keep the story going. But it was nip and tuck all the way, a very close call. Here's what happened.

They had jumped me and had me pinned to the ground and things were looking just about as bleak as things can look, when all at once, who or whom do you suppose came blundering into the picture?

Not Slim. No, not Uncle Johnny. He was probably asleep in his pickup. No, not the cattle rustler.

Missy Coyote? Nope.

You're not doing so well. Guess again. Not Loper.

Wallace and Junior? Not even close.

You give up? I knew you'd never guess. Okay, here's the answer: Brewster. Yes, good old sleepy-eyed Brewster. You'd completely forgotten about him, hadn't you?

Well, here he came, trotting up to the scene of the riot in that long bouncing stride of his, and with a big friendly grin all over his mouth.

"Oh, here you are. Gosh, I must have fallen asleep and when I woke up, you were gone, but here you are, I reckon."

Yes, there I was—on my back on the ground, being mauled and slobbered on by starving cannibals. Old Brew lumbered up to us and the first thing that happened was that he stepped right in the middle of Snort's face.

"Oops, 'scuse me."

Then he shifted his position to avoid Snort, and mashed Rip's nose three inches into the ground.

"Oops, sorry about that."

You know, there's one thing you never want to

do to a cannibal: step on his face. Brew had just done it twice, and with the biggest feet of any dog I'd ever seen before, I mean they were huge feet, and suddenly we had us two inflamed coyote brothers snarling at Brewster.

Well, let's put it this way. First they snarled, then their eyes bugged out of their heads when they began to realize how big he was.

He gave them his big sloppy grin. "How y'all tonight?"

He should have guessed that they weren't so good. I mean, not only were their eyes blazing with yellow fire but Rip had a dirt pile on the end of his nose where it had been buried in the ground, and Snort's left eye was beginning to swell shut.

"Not step on coyote face, big dummy!"

Brew seemed shocked. He turned to me (I was scraping myself off the ground), he turned to me and said, "Who are those boys talking to?"

In the process of turning, he also began to wag his tail. Have we discussed Brewster's tail? That thing was as big around as a tree limb, and fellers when he turned and wagged at the same time, that tail caught both coyote brothers right on the point of the chin and DECKED 'EM. I mean, lifted 'em off the ground and flipped 'em over backward.

If I'd started a right uppercut over in the next pasture and swung it with everything I had, it wouldn't have done half as much damage as what Brew had just done by accident.

That guy was dangerous, and the scary part was that he didn't even know it! He was still looking around with that puzzled grin on his face when Rip and Snort climbed off the floor.

"Have you caught the rustlers yet?"

"Uh no, not yet, Brew. I ran into a little snag."

"Aw heck. What happened?"

The brothers shook the stars and checkers out of their heads and prepared for action. I saw what was coming. "Brew, what snagged me is fixing to snag you. Check out your right flank."

Brew swung his head around just as Rip made a dive for him. Their heads collided in midair—CLUNK!—and Rip was bedded down for the rest of the evening. He hit the ground and didn't move a hair.

"Oops, 'scuse me there, sorry."

That made it one down and one to go, and the one to go looked madder than a den of bumblebees. He opened his coyote jaws to the fully open position (a pretty scary sight, in case you've never seen it), sprang through the air, and lit right in the middle of Brewster's back.

He delivered enough of a blow to cause Brewster to grunt and look around. "Hey, fella, take it easy, I've got a bad back." And just as though he were shooing a fly away, he threw an elbow that landed under Snort's chin and knocked him tail-over-teakettle out into the pasture.

Brew turned back to me and sniffed his nose. "Who are those guys? I never saw 'em before."

I dragged myself off the ground. "Just a couple of junior thugs who thought they were pretty tough until they tangled with you. And me, of course. We make a pretty awesome team, Brew."

"Thanks, Hank."

"I could have whipped 'em but it would have taken me a lot longer if you hadn't come along. You . . . that is, WE sure cleaned house on those guys."

"You mean . . . that was a fight?"

"Oh, just a little altercation, nothing to write home about."

"I don't much go in for fightin'."

"Yeah, well, the way you operate, you probably don't get a whole lot of practice."

"No sir, I don't believe in violence. Heck, if you can't work things out by talking, you ought to just walk away from it, is how I've always looked at it."

"Right."

I crept to the top of the hill and studied the situation down below. The rustler had finished closing in the corral with the portable panels and had made himself a little chute that led into the trailer. He was inside the pen with five or six cow-calf pairs, trying to get the calves to load.

It appeared that he wasn't having much luck, which meant that we might have enough time to run back to camp and alert Slim to what was

going on. That was kind of important to solving the case, don't you see, because only Slim could write down the description of the vehicle and the license number.

I do many things well, but writing down license numbers isn't one of them.

"Well, Brew, our next assignment is to highball it back to camp and get Slim out of bed."

His ears jumped and his eyes grew wide. "Did you say 'highball it back to camp?'"

"That's correct, at top speed."

He plunked his big bohunkus down on the ground. "You know, Hank, I've never been too keen on highballing it back to anywhere, and if it's all the same to you, I think I'll stick around here and try to keep this hill from blowing away. And I might even," he yawned, "take me a little nap."

"What'll you do when Rip and Snort wake up?"

"Who? Oh, them? Shucks, they seemed like pretty nice fellers to me, just a little clumsy, is all. I don't think we'll have any trouble."

I glanced at the sleeping cannibals. Brewster would probably never realize that he had just thrashed two of the toughest coyotes in Ochiltree County, and I didn't see any point in trying to explain it to him. But I couldn't help wondering how much damage the guy could do if he ever tried.

"All right, you stay here and keep your eye on that rustler, and I'll make a lightning dash back to camp."

"Good deal. You handle the lightning dashes, and I'll sure keep my eyes on the rustler—if I can keep 'em open that long, is where the problem's going to come." He yawned again. "Boy, you guard dogs don't wrinkle the sheets much at night, do you?"

"Just part of the job, Brewster."

"Yep, and I'm sure glad it's your job and not mine." He crossed his paws in front of him and laid his chin on the crossed paws. "Holler when you need me, otherwise I'll zzzzzzzzzz."

It sure didn't take him long to fall asleep. He may very well have been the sleepingest dog I'd ever run across.

Well, maybe Brewster had time to take a nap but I sure didn't. I pointed myself toward the northeast, hit Code Three, and went streaking up the canyon.

I won't go into details about my emergency run back to camp—how I leaped over rocks and fallen trees, climbed mountains and swam swollen rivers, ran through brambles and sticker weeds and thissy thornals . . . thorny thistles, that is; whipped twenty-two head of hungry coyotes, two badgers, and three porcupines.

I won't mention any of that, or how I arrived

back at camp, exhausted, spent, completely used up, battered, on my last leg, near death, but triumphant through it all.

I'll say only that I made it back to camp, staggered up to the tent flap, and began barking the alarm.

"Hank, shut up!"

He didn't understand. This wasn't just ordinary late-night barking, but rather a Code Three situation that demanded his immediate attention, so I turned up the volume and barked harder and louder than . . .

SPLAT!

Was he trying to be funny? Throwing pillows at the Head of Ranch Security in the middle of the night? What kind of outfit was this, anyway?

Hey, we didn't have a minute to spare! That rustler was down there loading cattle, and if I didn't get Slim out of bed pretty quick . . .

I had to do something to wake him up, and do it fast. I did.

CHAPTER TWELVE

Another Triumph Over the Crinimal Forces

I would have preferred not to bite his toes, but he had left me with no choice. They were exposed, don't you see, and sticking out from under his blanket.

"EEEEEEE-YOW!"

I hated to do it, but by George it worked. He flew out of that bed and chased me around the tent three times trying to perform some act of violence upon me, but on the third lap he finally woke up.

"Holy smokes, are you trying to tell me something, Hank?"

Right. There's a cow thief in the pasture and

you're chasing me around the tent, and don't we look foolish?

"Do we have a cow thief in the pasture?"

I barked.

It takes a lot of patience to work with these cowboys, but if you stay after them and don't get shot or strangled or clubbed to death with a pillow, they'll eventually come around.

I had never thought of Slim as being a guy who moved with lightning speed, mainly because on an ordinary day he moved with nonlightning speed. In other words, no speed at all.

Very slowly. Like a turtle or a waterdog or a wounded goose.

But once he figgered out what was going on, he jumped into his clothes, grabbed up a bridle, ran down to the grassy flat where the horses were hobbled and grazing, caught old Dunny, stuffed the bit into his mouth, and swung up on his back.

He didn't take the time to saddle Dunny, but rode him bareback. Now, that was more like it. At last we were getting some action out of the cowboy crew.

"Come on, pup. Lead the way."

And so it was that we went streaking down the canyon, with me out front in the lead position, leaping rocks and fallen trees, climbing rivers and

swimming swollen mountains, and so forth. I won't go into all the details.

How did I do it? How could ANY dog made of mere flesh and blood and hair and bones accomplish so many incredible, impossible feats in one night? All I can tell you is that it couldn't be done, but I did it anyway.

Okay, by the time we reached the south end of

the pasture, Slim could see the headlights. He left Dunny hobbled in the bottom of the draw and climbed to the top of the hill—with me leading the way, of course.

When we got there, we looked down into the next draw and . . . I couldn't believe that Brewster was down there, *helping the rustler load up the last of the calves!*

Well, maybe he wasn't exactly helping. I had already picked up on the fact that Brewster had about as much cow-sense as your average lumber truck, so he couldn't have been much help, even if he'd wanted to. But he sure as thunder wasn't doing anything to stop the crime from happening.

I mean, he was trotting along beside the rustler, panting happily and wagging his tree-limb tail. And get this. When the rustler had loaded up all his portable corral panels and was ready to go, Brewster hopped up into the back of the pickup, just as though they had become the best of friends!

When I asked him about this later, he said, "Stealing Uncle Johnny's cattle? Aw heck, is that what he was doing? He sure seemed like a nice feller to me."

I guess if the rustler hadn't kicked him out and told him to go home, Brewster would have become an outlaw dog, and probably never would have known the difference, since he slept most of the time anyway. If you're always asleep, it doesn't make much difference which side of the law you're on.

Well, the rustler was a slick operator, but he made one little mistake (they always do, you know). He should have disconnected the lights on his license plates. But he didn't. Slim got a good look at the tags on the trailer and the pickup, and wrote the numbers down in the palm of his hand.

"His goose is now cooked," said Slim with a smile. "Let's see, this is Wednesday. He'll be taking them calves to the livestock auction in Beaver. I have an idea that old Chumpy Cates of the Cattle Raisers will be waiting for him at the sale barn when he backs up to the chute."

And that's pretty muchly the way things turned out. Slim climbed on Dunny and rode the two miles down to Loper's hay field, where he was baling the hay he'd mowed the day before. They drove to the house and put in a call to Chumpy Cates in Canadian (got him out of bed, I'll bet).

And with that, the wheels of justice began to roll.

When daylight came, Slim and Loper combed the pasture on horseback and found Uncle Johnny's pickup, right where he had parked it in a washout.

(I found him, actually, but don't expect the cowboys to remember it that way.)

Uncle Johnny was spread out across the seat, with his boots sticking out the window and his head pillowed on a rolled-up gunnysack. Slim and Loper woke him up by banging on the hood of the pickup and yelling, "Hey, wake up in there! You're parked in a fire lane and we're fixing to tow your vehicle!"

Always making jokes, those two. How I manage to run this ranch with . . . oh well.

Uncle Johnny came out wearing a sheepish grin. "I figgered you old boys would find me sooner or later. Sure enough, it was later. Has anybody seen my dog? Brewster quit me after the wreck and I ain't seen him since. I hope the coyotes didn't eat him."

Coyotes? Eat Brewster? Ho, that was a laugh! Who can eat a dog that's always stepping in your face? Rip and Snort would have gotten a big chuckle out of that.

As a matter of fact, Brewster had already reclaimed his spot in the back of Uncle Johnny's pickup and was throwing up a big long line of Z's.

Well, Slim and Loper tied onto Uncle Johnny's pickup with ropes and horses and pulled it out of the wash, and then we all headed down to headquarters for coffee and the ritual known as "The Telling of Tales."

Gathered in Sally May's backyard, we all listened as Slim told and retold of our adventures up in the canyon. And yes, even I was admitted into the yard—under a temporary visa, you might say—although I could hardly relax and enjoy myself with Sally May standing nearby.

I went out of my way to smile and wag my tail at her, but she was bad about holding a grudge, you might remember, and I found it convenient to, uh, camp beneath Slim's chair and cast glances at her from afar, so to speak.

Reading the expression on her face from afar, I certainly got the feeling that my temporary visa would be very temporary, and that if I so much as set foot in her flower beds, I would feel the sting of her tongue, and then of her broom.

Slim told about how he'd gotten bucked off his horse—although he neglected to say that it happened TWICE, not once. It appeared that this event would end up as one of those secrets between a cowboy and his dog.

Too bad we dogs can't talk. If we could, it would add a whole new dimension to mankind's knowledge of cowboys.

Then he told his "Weenie Thief" story and it

was greeted with howls of laughter. Even Sally May loosened up enough to crack a smile and say something like, "Don't I know that dog?" Then he told the "Tent Rope" story, and I thought Uncle Johnny would fall out of his chair laughing.

I missed the humor of it myself.

But then Slim scratched me behind the ears. "Nice work, Hank. I hate to give you credit for anything, you're such a goof-off, but this time you did come through in the clutch. You ate my weenies, but then you saved my bacon. Say, that would make a great country song, wouldn't it?"

Well . . . I wasn't so sure that would make a "great country song," and he had certainly given me a mixed compliment, to say the least. I didn't know what he meant by that "goof-off" business, and as for the slur about me stealing his alleged weenies . . .

Hey, I still held firm to the theory that those weenies had simply disappeared from camp. Vanished without a trace. Probably misplaced by some careless person.

A simple case of mistaken identity.

On the other hand, a guy takes his roses when and however he can, and Slim had definitely hit a bull's-eye in giving me full and total credit for cracking the Case of the Midnight Rustler.

And I did enjoy a moment of glory, there in Sally May's precious yard, in the golden light of dawn. Perhaps the most moving part of the whole ceremony came when Sally May herself said, "Well, I had my chance to murder the nasty thing, but maybe it's a good thing that I didn't do it."

And with that my visa expired and I was invited to leave the yard—which was sure okay with me.

And while they laughed and told windy tales and drank coffee, guess who slipped back into harness and went back to work, protecting his ranch from evil forces.

ME.

I had cracked another case and had produced another happy ending, had even managed to squeeze a little appreciation out of certain unnamed persons whose names I won't mention. And fellers, that's as good as it gets around here.

Case closed, and back to work.

Have you read all of Hank's adventures?

Join Hank the Cowdog's Security Force

Are you a big Hank the Cowdog fan? Then you'll want to join Hank's Security Force. Here is some of the neat stuff you will receive:

Welcome Package
- A Hank paperback embossed with Hank's top secret seal
- Free Hank bookmarks

Eight issues of *The Hank Times* with
- Stories about Hank and his friends
- Lots of great games and puzzles
- Special previews of future books
- Fun contests

More Security Force Benefits
- Special discounts on Hank books and audiotapes
- An original Hank poster (19" x 25") absolutely free
- Unlimited access to Hank's Security Force website at www.hankthecowdog.com

Total value of the Welcome Package and *The Hank Times* is $23.95. However, your two year membership is only **$8.95** plus $3.00 for shipping and handling.

To join Hank's Security Force, please send a check or money order for $11.95 ($8.95 plus $3.00 shipping and handling), payable to Maverick Books, to:

Hank's Security Force
Maverick Books
P.O. Box 549
Perryton, Texas 79070

Be sure to include your name, address, phone number, and your choice of a free book (choose from any book in the series). Please include two choices in case your first choice is out of stock.

DO NOT SEND CASH. NO CREDIT CARDS ACCEPTED.
Allow 4–6 weeks for delivery.

The Hank the Cowdog Security Force, the Welcome Package, and The Hank Times *are the sole responsibility of Maverick Books. They are not organized, sponsored, or endorsed by Penguin Putnam Inc., Puffin Books, Viking Children's Books, or their subsidiaries or affiliates.*

Visit the fan club website at
www.hankthecowdog.com

John R. Erickson

began writing stories in 1967 while working full-time as a cowboy, farmhand, and ranch manager in Texas and Oklahoma—where two of the dogs were Hank and his sidekick Drover. Hank the Cowdog made his debut a long time ago in the pages of *The Cattleman*, a magazine about cattle for adults. Soon after, Erickson began receiving "Dear Hank" letters and realized that many of his eager fans were children.

The Hank the Cowdog series won Erickson a *Publishers Weekly* "Listen Up" Award for Best Humor in Audio. He also received an Audie from the Audio Publishers Association for Outstanding Children's Series.

The author of more than thirty-five books, Erickson lives with his wife, Kris, and their three children on a ranch near his boyhood home of Perryton, Texas.

Gerald L. Holmes

met John Erickson after moving to Perryton, Texas, a long time ago . . . and that's when Hank and his pals came to life for the first time in pictures. Mr. Holmes has illustrated numerous cartoons and textbooks in addition to the Hank the Cowdog series.

11/13/18: Water damage noted
throughout the book.
WGRL-HQ SC

The case of the midnight rustler /
J FIC ERICK   31057001930703

Erickson, John R.,
WEST GA REGIONAL LIBRARY SYS